The Kid and the Chameleon Sleepover

Also by Sheri Mabry

The Kid and the Chameleon

The Kid and the Chameleon Sleepover

Sheri Mabry

illustrated by Joanie Stone

Albert Whitman & Company
Chicago, Illinois

For Brinkey, Hudson, and Hartley: may your lives be
filled with beautiful friendships—SM

To John and Yvette—JS

Library of Congress Cataloging-in-Publication data is on file with the publisher.

Text copyright © 2019 by Sheri Mabry
Illustrations copyright © 2019 by Albert Whitman & Company
Illustrations by Joanie Stone
First published in the United States of America
in 2019 by Albert Whitman & Company
ISBN 978-0-8075-4180-7
Printed in China
10 9 8 7 6 5 4 3 2 1 WKT 22 21 20 19 18

Design by Morgan Beck

For more information about Albert Whitman & Company,
visit our website at www.albertwhitman.com.

100 Years of Albert Whitman & Company
Celebrate with us in 2019!

Chapter One

A chameleon sat on a leaf.

He looked down. He saw a kid.

A kid sat on a log.

She looked up. She saw a chameleon.

"Newton! It's *you*!" said the girl.

"I am always me, Tessy," said the chameleon.

"You're invited to my sleepover tonight," said Tessy.

"What's a sleepover?" asked Newton. "It does not sound like a chameleon thing."

"It's a kid thing," said Tessy. "We can have fun, you'll see."

"You are a kid. I am a chameleon," said Newton. "I'm not making any promises."

Chapter Two

The sun began to go down. The moon
began to rise.

"Time for the sleepover!" said Tessy.
She scooped Newton up.

"I was already sleeping," said Newton.
"Please put me down."

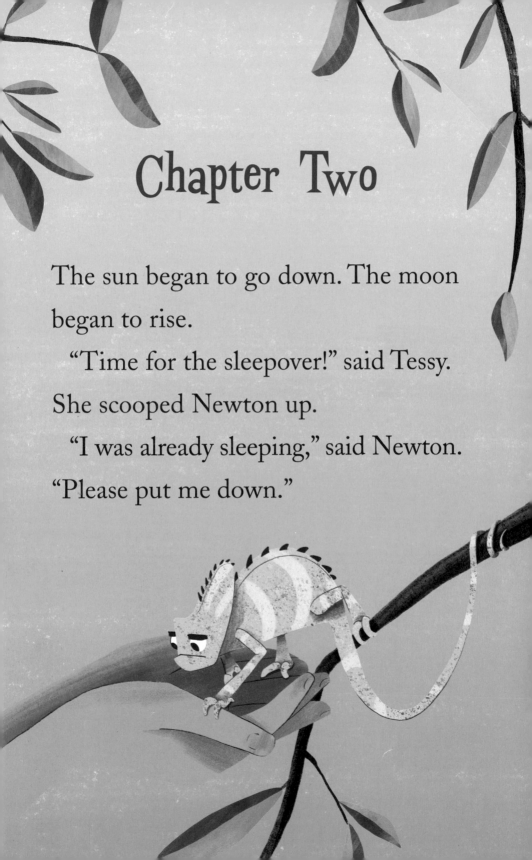

Tessy took Newton inside. They went to the kitchen. She put Newton down. "Let's start with snacks!" she said. "Snacks are a part of a sleepover."

"What if no one is hungry?" asked Newton.

"Everyone is always hungry for snacks at a sleepover," said Tessy. "It's a sleepover thing."

Tessy got out the peanut butter.
She put out the raisins. She washed
the celery.

"These are called ants on a log,"
she said.

Newton flicked his tongue for
a taste. He took a bite.

"*BLAH!*" said Newton, spitting it out. "Those are not ants! And that is not a log!" Newton turned brown. He stuck his head out the window.

"What are you doing?" asked Tessy.

Newton's tongue flicked.

It flicked.

It flicked again.

"Having *real* ants on a log,"
he said.

"ICK!" said Tessy. "Those are bugs! Those are not a sleepover snack!"

"There are *rules* to a sleepover?" said Newton. "I'm losing interest."

He shut one eye. Then the other.

"Buuurp!"

Chapter Three

"Time to play a game," said Tessy.
"Let's have a pillow fight!"

"Fighting is not my thing,"
said Newton.

"It's with pillows," said Tessy.
"Pillow fighting is everyone's thing
at a sleepover."

"What is a pillow?" asked Newton.

"It's soft and squishy," said Tessy.

"Soft and squishy?" said Newton.

"*Mmm.* Sounds like a snack!
A snack that a chameleon would like.
I'll take one!"

Tessy laughed. She tossed Newton
a pillow. His tongue flicked. He took
a bite.

"*Blah*! That is *not* a chameleon
snack," said Newton.

"No, it is not a snack," said Tessy.
"It's for a pillow fight, like I said."

Newton turned bright colors.

"Whoa, what is going on?" said Tessy. "You have turned colors! Beautiful!"

"Not beautiful," said Newton. "I'm scary! Bright colors are *scary*! This is how chameleons fight—with bright colors!" said Newton. "Still, it is *not* a chameleon thing to fight pillows."

"Then let's try hide-and-seek. You will hide. I will seek. *Go!*"

Tessy covered her eyes.

Newton yawned.

"One, two, three…," said Tessy.

"Why are you counting?" asked Newton. "We are playing hide-and-seek. Not math."

"When I get to ten, I will come and find you," said Tessy. "Four, five, six…"

"I need quiet," said Newton. "You are keeping me awake."

"I have to count," said Tessy. "It's a kid rule. Besides, we are playing hide-and-*seek*, not hide-and-*sleep*."

Newton covered his ear holes.
He closed his eyes. He took deep
breaths. He turned soft colors and
blended in.

"Seven, eight, nine, ten!" said Tessy.
"Ready or not, here I come!"

Tessy opened her eyes.

She looked under books. "Where are you?" she asked.

Newton didn't answer.

Tessy looked in a drawer. "Give me a hint," she said.

Newton blinked.

"Tell me where you are!" yelled Tessy.

Nothing.

"This is too hard," she said. "I give up!"

Newton flicked his tongue. "Here," he said. "I'm here."

"That's not fair!" said Tessy. "You turned colors so I couldn't see you. You broke the rules."

"It is fair," said Newton. "Changing colors might not be a kid rule, but it is a chameleon rule.

"Anyway, I thought this was about sleeping," said Newton. "When is it time to sleep?"

Chapter Four

"I changed into pajamas, Newton. You should change into your pajamas too."

"I change colors. Not clothes," said Newton.

"Then it's time to brush our teeth," said Tessy.

She gave Newton the toothpaste.

"What am I supposed to do with this?" asked Newton.

"Brush your teeth with it," said Tessy.

"I don't have a brush," said Newton. "More to the point, I don't have teeth."

"Then wash your face," said Tessy.

Newton blinked. "My face isn't dirty," said Newton.

"Then scrub behind your ears," said Tessy.

"No can do," said Newton. "I don't have ear flaps like you."

"Fine, then we will read a bedtime story," said Tessy.

"*Hmm*," said Newton. "I only read chameleon."

"No problem," said Tessy. "I'll make up a story instead. An adventure sleepover story!"

"Once upon a time, there was a kid," said Tessy.

"The kid was strong and brave and loved adventures. One day, she saved a lonely chameleon from a big scary spider. When she kissed the chameleon, he turned into a—"

"Did you say she kissed the chameleon?" yelled Newton. "Blah!

"That is *not* a story for a chameleon. *This* is how the story goes. Once upon a time, there was a chameleon. The chameleon was smart and funny and clever.

"One day, he saw a kid. She was
sitting on a rock. So…He crawled up
a tree and took a nap."

"A nap?!" said Tessy. "That is *so* boring! This isn't an adventure story! This is *not* a story for a sleepover."

"It is for me," said Newton. "It's about sleeping." He shut one eye. He shut the other. He began to snore.

"Hey, wake up," said Tessy.

"Why?" asked Newton. "I thought the point of a sleepover was to sleep!" Newton rubbed his eyes. He flicked his tongue. He fell asleep.

Chapter Five

Newton opened one eye. He opened the other.

"You want to have a sleepover? I'll show you how to have a sleepover," he said. "Follow me."

Tessy followed.

"Lay there," said Newton.

"On this rock?" asked Tessy. "But it's buggy out, and it's dark out!

"Exactly!" said Newton, crawling farther down the branch.

Tessy laid down
on the rock.

She rolled off.

She tried again.

She rolled
off again.

"Newton, sleepovers are supposed to have snacks, fun games, and bedtime stories! We were supposed to tell secrets to each other! And Newton, kids do *not* like sleeping on rocks. This is *not* how kids have sleepovers."

"Exactly," said Newton. "You are a kid. I am a chameleon. What did you expect?"

"I expected a *SLEEPOVER!*" said Tessy.

"I am sleeping," Newton looked down, "over…you. This *is* a sleepover. Chameleon style."

Tessy crossed her arms. She rolled off the rock. "Well, it is *not* working for me."

Newton turned brown. "It's not my thing either!" he said. "It's past my bedtime. Raisins are sour. And I don't like fighting pillows!"

"Night," said Tessy. She stomped
back inside.

"Night," mumbled Newton. He
crawled farther up the branch.

Chapter Six

Newton lay alone in a tree. He wrapped himself with his tail.

Tessy lay alone in her room. She wrapped herself with her blanket.

Newton ate bugs.

Tessy drank a cup of water.

Tessy finally fell asleep.

Newton snored.

The morning sun peeked in Tessy's room.

Newton peeked in Tessy's room.

"Wake up!" said Newton.

Tessy yawned. "What is it?"

"The sleepover thing wasn't exactly for me," said Newton. "But it *did* work."

"What do you mean?" said Tessy. "You slept in a tree. I slept in my house. The sleepover didn't work."

"It did work," said Newton. "If we call it a sleep's over!"

"Oh, I get it!" giggled Tessy.
"A sleep's over because the sleep is
now over! And now we can have a
whole day of fun!"

"Do you mean chameleon fun or kid
fun?" asked Newton.

"Friends fun," said Tessy.

Newton flicked his tongue and turned orange. "Maybe we can," he said.

Newton climbed onto Tessy's shoulder. He crawled into a soft curl.

Tessy packed kid snacks and gathered chameleon snacks.

"Tessy?" said Newton.

"What Newton?" said Tessy.

"I have lots of chameleon secrets to share with you!" he said, flicking his tongue.

"I have lots of kid secrets to share with you!" said Tessy, laughing.

Then Newton and Tessy set off on a day full of adventures…together.

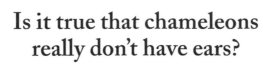

Chameleon Facts

Is it true that chameleons really don't have ears?

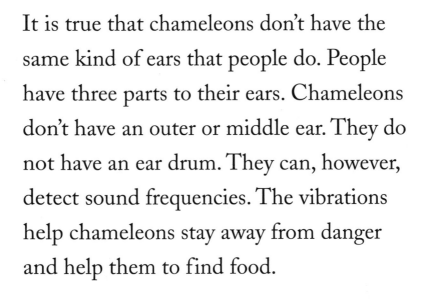

It is true that chameleons don't have the same kind of ears that people do. People have three parts to their ears. Chameleons don't have an outer or middle ear. They do not have an ear drum. They can, however, detect sound frequencies. The vibrations help chameleons stay away from danger and help them to find food.